This book is dedicated to
Christina, Mavis and Charlie Mogotsi
who lived in a shelter
for six years.

First published 1989 in Southern Africa
by Songololo Books
a division of David Philip Publishers (Pty) Ltd
208 Werdmuller Centre, Claremont 7700

This edition published 1991 by
Walker Books Ltd, 87 Vauxhall Walk
London SE11 5HJ

Text © 1989 Reviva Schermbrucker
Illustrations © 1989 Niki Daly

Printed and bound in Hong Kong
by Dai Nippon Printing Co. (H. K.) Ltd

British Library Cataloguing in Publication Data
Schermbrucker, Reviva
Charlie's house.
I. Title
823

ISBN 0-7445-1519-X

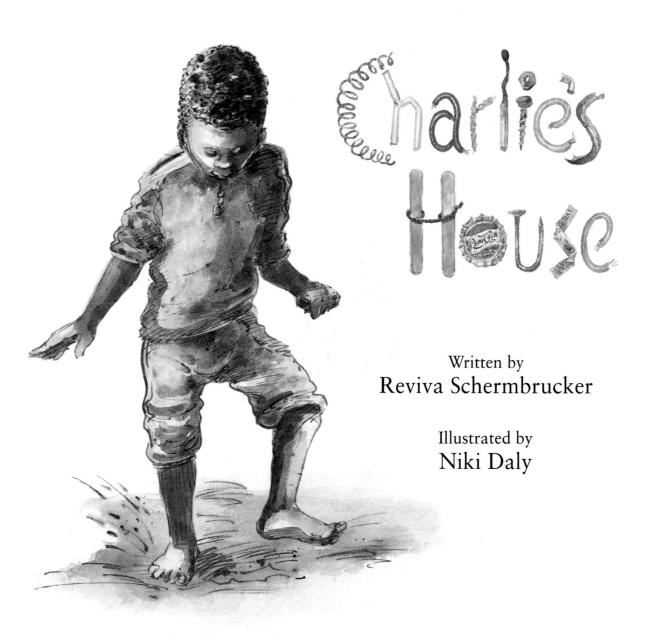

Charlie's House

Written by
Reviva Schermbrucker

Illustrated by
Niki Daly

WALKER BOOKS
LONDON

In the backyard of a house in Guguletu was a shelter made of corrugated iron and scrap, with two small windows and a single door.

This is where Charlie Mogotsi lived
with his mother and granny.

One summer, Charlie watched the men build the shelter.
First they laid a cement floor and placed a pole
in each corner.

Then they built the walls and roof with iron sheets
and very long nails.

His mother was angry with the builders because
the roof did not fit properly and some of the iron
sheets had holes in them.

Next winter, Charlie watched his mother move
the furniture and place pots on the cement floor to
catch the leaks. She sighed while the water dripped.

When the rain stopped, Charlie played in a muddy
furrow between the rows of houses. He began to
build. First he stamped down a mud floor and put
a stick in each corner.

Then he built the walls with rough clay sausages
which he lined with cardboard scraps.

He made the rooms big. One was a lounge where his granny could entertain her friends and watch TV.

Another, a bedroom with twin beds for his
mother and granny.

But one was a bedroom all for himself!

Charlie also built a kitchen and put in a milk-carton fridge. Then he made an indoor bathroom, where he put a plastic bottle split in half by the sun. When it was filled with water it made a lovely bath for builders to wash off all the mud.

Next he patted and squeezed a handful of clay into a sofa and chairs. Then he polished a tabletop with some water. For carpets, Charlie lay down strips from a plastic bag.

On the rooftop he put a forked twig as a TV aerial and in the backyard a washing-line made from a scrap of wool and two lolly-sticks.

Charlie was busy modelling the rich curves of a car when he heard his granny calling, "Charlie! Your mother is home from work."

Charlie sat down to a meal of bread and soup with his mother and granny. Carefully he bit two mouthfuls from the centre of his bread and balanced the slice on his nose.

He dreamt he was wearing sunglasses and driving his very own car past the house that he had just built. "Don't play with your food. Eat up," said his granny.

But Charlie dreamed on. He put his foot down ...

and kept on going.